Acting Edition

Regretfully, So the Birds Are

by Julia Izumi

SAMUEL FRENCH

FOR PRODUCTION INQUIRIES

UNITED STATES AND CANADA
info@concordtheatricals.com
1-866-979-0447

UNITED KINGDOM AND EUROPE
licensing@concordtheatricals.co.uk
020-7054-7298

Each title is subject to availability from Concord Theatricals Corp., depending upon country of performance. Please be aware that *REGRETFULLY, SO THE BIRDS ARE* may not be licensed by Concord Theatricals Corp. in your territory. Professional and amateur producers should contact the nearest Concord Theatricals Corp. office or licensing partner to verify availability.

This work is published by Samuel French, an imprint of Concord Theatricals Corp.

No one shall make any changes in this title(s) for the purpose of production. No part of this book may be reproduced, stored in a retrieval system, scanned, uploaded, or transmitted in any form, by any means, now known or yet to be invented, including mechanical, electronic, digital, photocopying, recording, videotaping, or otherwise, without the prior written permission of the publisher. No one shall share this title(s), or any part of this title(s), through any social media or file hosting websites.

For all inquiries regarding motion picture, television, online/digital and other media rights, please contact Concord Theatricals Corp.

MUSIC AND THIRD-PARTY MATERIALS USE NOTE

Licensees are solely responsible for obtaining formal written permission from copyright owners to use copyrighted music and/or other copyrighted third-party materials (e.g. artworks, logos) in the performance of this play and are strongly cautioned to do so. If no such permission is obtained by the licensee, then the licensee must use only original music and materials that the licensee owns and controls. Licensees are solely responsible and liable for clearances of all third-party copyrighted materials, including without limitation music, and shall indemnify the copyright owners of the play(s) and their licensing agent, Concord Theatricals Corp., against any costs, expenses, losses and liabilities arising from the use of such copyrighted third-party materials by licensees. For music, please contact the appropriate music licensing authority in your territory for the rights to any incidental music.

IMPORTANT BILLING AND CREDIT REQUIREMENTS

If you have obtained performance rights to this title, please refer to your licensing agreement for important billing and credit requirements.

REGRETFULLY, SO THE BIRDS ARE was first produced by Playwrights Horizons (Adam Greenfield, Artistic Director; Leslie Marcus, Managing Director) and WP Theater (Lisa McNulty, Artistic Director; Michael Sag, Managing Director) in New York City on April 11, 2023. The performance was directed by Jenny Koons and assistant directed by Raecine Singletary, with sets by You-Shin Chen, costumes by Alicia J. Austin, lighting by Stacey Derosier, sound by Megumi Katayama, and props by Matt Carlin. The Production Stage Manager was Jenny Kennedy, the Assistant Stage Manager was Jessie Moore, and the Stage Management Fellow was Carter White. The cast was as follows:

ILLY	Sasha Diamond
NEEL	Sky Smith
MORA	Shannon Tyo
ELINORE	Kristine Nielsen
CAM THE SNOWMAN	Gibson Frazier
SREY	Pearl Sun

REGRETFULLY, SO THE BIRDS ARE was developed at the 2021 Ojai Playwrights Conference (Robert Egan, Artistic Director/Producer).

CHARACTERS

ILLY – 25, female, Asian American

NEEL – 28, male, Asian American

MORA – 29 going on 30, female, Asian American

ELINORE – 62, female, white American

CAM THE SNOWMAN – an American snow(white)man

SREY – age unclear, female, Cambodian?

COWMAN – male, played by same actor as **CAM THE SNOWMAN**

A BIRD – very bird, played by same actor as **ELINORE**

MANY BIRDS – so very birds, played by **EVERYBODY!**

SETTING

A half-burnt home in New Jersey with a treehouse and a snowman outside, a jail visitation room, an airport in Guangzhou, China, somewhere in Nebraska, others?

AUTHOR'S NOTES

Lines in brackets within a different character's line should be spoken aloud while the person whose actual line it is continues over it.

These characters have no subtext.

This play is a farcical tragedy.

NOTE ON MUSIC

Sheet music for **ILLY**'s songs on pages 10 and 35 as well as the song sung by the **BIRDS** on page 69 are provided at the end of the script. A karaoke track for said **BIRDS**' song, referred to on page 60, is available for use and can be licensed from Concord, but you may invent your own.

ACT ONE: Dramatic Family

Scene i

*(**ILLY** and **NEEL** are sitting in a treehouse.)*

*(**ILLY** is pointing to clouds in the sky.)*

ILLY. That one
And that one
And that one
And that one
And the one that looks like mushrooms. Or maybe
they're hands?

NEEL. What about those birds?

ILLY. I don't think so, they weren't in the paperwork.
But all those clouds
And all the space in between them
Are alllll mine.

> *(She points to **NEEL**.)*

And you. You're all mine too. Even though you're also
not in the paperwork.

NEEL. So the birds get to be free but I have to be yours,
huh?

ILLY. Yeah. What're you gonna do about it?

NEEL. I got some ideas...

> *(He whispers something in her ear. She giggles.)*

Wow. You have a part of the sky. I get to sit in this
treehouse, point right there and say, "that's Illy's sky."

ILLY. That's my sky. A sky made just for me. I earned it.

(They sit in a lovey-dovey [pun-intended] silence.)

(Suddenly, a bird screeches.)

Scene ii

(**CAM THE SNOWMAN** *is standing in a yard, as would any snowman.*)

CAM THE SNOWMAN. Some fun facts:

Pol Pot got married in 1956.

Cam Whistler got married in the snow.

Pol Pot taught history, geography and French literature from 1956 to 1963 at a private school in Cambodia while simultaneously plotting a revolution.

Cam Whistler taught Asian History from ages thirty-one to sixty-three at a community college in New Jersey while simultaneously raising three children.

None of this stuff will be on the exam, but it might get you extra credit.

Scene iii

(A couch.)

*(**MORA** sits on it with her head in her hands.)*

*(**ILLY** and **NEEL** stand in front of her, staring.)*

(Silence for some time.)

*(Finally **MORA** takes a deep breath and lifts her head.)*

MORA. But didn't you think
For one second
That we weren't, like,
Fucked up enough?
That, like,
I wasn't fucked up enough?

> *(**ILLY** maybe rolls her eyes or mumbles something about how this isn't about her.)*

NEEL. But that's exactly why this is great! I mean, look at us, Mora! Look at our current circumstances:

When you're an Asian adoptee whose parents won't let you or your adopted siblings know what country you each separately come from, and you're also a human disaster who lives in your childhood New Jersey home because you can't keep a job and you keep getting dumped, and your pill-popping mom is awaiting trial for arson and manslaughter for setting your dad on fire because he cheated on her multiple times, does your genetically unrelated brother and sister being in love with each other really seem that bad?

MORA. ...

...

Yeah. [**NEEL**. Wow I guess I really called that one wrong.]
I mean I don't even know where to begin with this—
like this is crazy, right?? You both gotta admit this is
crazy??

NEEL. C'mon Mora, deep down, you gotta have seen this
coming.

MORA. Who would see this coming.

NEEL. Well Illy and I have always had this weird tension.

MORA. I have a weird tension, Neel.
In my left foot.
But I let it go.
That's what you do with weird tensions.
You let them go.
Or you get a massage.
Why couldn't you get a massage instead of having an
affair.

ILLY. We're not having an affair.

MORA. You just told me that you're—

ILLY. One of us has to be married for us to have an affair.
And we're not married.

MORA. You're not.
You're not getting married.
You're never getting married, right?

(**ILLY** *and* **NEEL** *have an awkward look.*)

NEEL. Uhhhhh, well—

MORA. (*Convulses in disgust.*) AH, ew, EyAuW~, stop—
stop whatever—get away just get OUT GET AWAY
RIGHT NOW RIGHT NOW.

(**ILLY** *and* **NEEL** *start to leave.*)

WAIT!

(ILLY and NEEL wait.)

MORA. ....when......?
When did...
When—

NEEL. When did the weird tension start?

MORA. No.
Yes.
I dunno.
Yes.

(ILLY and NEEL hesitate.)

TELL ME ABOUT YOUR WEIRD TENSION GO GO
GO—

ILLY. Remember when we would go to Mrs. Bashar's
house for Thanksgiving and remember how we would
go in the yard with the other kids and you and the
other older kids would grab us by the wrist and spin
us around and you would always spin me around but
then that one year everyone thought you had shingles
and you stayed home so Neel tried to spin me and I
really didn't want him to but he grabbed my wrists and
he kept pulling me and I was like I hate this but then
I was like laughing and I looked at Neel and he was
laughing and pulling and then we both just stopped
because suddenly it was like...weird.

> *(A pause in which **MORA** is clenching her face
> trying to imagine but also not imagine the
> moment and **NEEL** is wondering if he should
> mention that this was not the moment he was
> thinking of.)*

MORA. ...I wasn't even there.

ILLY. What?

MORA. I wasn't even there for your first weird tension?

> (**ILLY** *makes a noise and gesture in frustration about* **MORA**'s *continued ability to make everything about her.*)

NEEL. I mean your presence always kind of made the tension less weird! Which is why things didn't really change between us until you left for college—

MORA. You're telling me this has been going on for over a DECADE?!?!?!

NEEL. Nothing actually happened until Illy was eighteen!!

MORA. Oh good! Now that I know you were both consenting adults, that makes this all TOTALLY FINE!!!!!!!!

> (*A silence with a weird tension.*)

Sorry.
As your older sister—
As your disaster older sister—
Who you've (almost) always supported—
I know I should—
I know I should probably, like, I guess, support?
You guys?
About...this...thing?
I'm just.
I'm gonna need a while to just.
To get used...?
To?
...

NEEL. You know, at the end of the day, we're not blood-related, so if it's easier to just think of us as—

> (**MORA** *throws a pillow from the couch towards* **NEEL** *who ducks right in time.*)

MORA. You did **NOT** just **FUCKING** say—

NEEL. I TAKE IT BACK! I TAKE IT BACK!

(*During the below* **MORA** *continues to throw pillows at* **NEEL** *who runs around the room trying to avoid getting hit and occasionally yelling "I'm sorry!" When she runs out of pillows on the couch she takes the couch back cushions and then the seat cushions and when it seems like she runs out of cushions, she reaches inside the couch and more appear.*)

MORA. Fifth grade. I come pick you up after practice. Gerry Alterman, human sewage that I can't believe you still hang out with, tells the coach that I wasn't allowed to, to pick you up, because what? Because we weren't real brother and sister—because we weren't [**NEEL & ILLY.** Blood-related!] BLOOD-RELATED and then you punched him in the face and broke your knuckles and THAT is the PROUDEST I have EVER been of you, Neel. And that was when we made a PACT, the first PACT of our Whistler Sibling PACTS—PACT NUMBER ONE that we would NEVER say that we weren't "blood-related" because we are just as siblings as any other siblings and you DARE fucking even try to fucking throw in my fucking face—

(**ILLY** *smacks* **MORA** *in the face with one of the thrown pillows [which was also probably a throw pillow. Ahaha].*)

ILLY. WE GET IT, MORA—Neel is sorry he said that, OKAY? And I'm sorry it's hard but we are all still siblings, we'll always be siblings, and Neel and I are also in a committed romantic relationship! Sometimes all of those things are just true, OKAY? If you would just shut up for two seconds, we can go over our plan for the future which—

MORA. I'm telling Mom you HIT MY FACE.

ILLY. You almost hit Neel in the face like five times!

MORA. He broke a Pact!

NEEL. I did break a Pact—

MORA. I'm gonna tell Mom you hit me in the face AND that you two are KISSING.

ILLY. You can't be the one to tell her—

NEEL. We do more than KISSING—!

MORA. ahhhhhhhh~

ILLY. SHUT UP, NEEL! *(To* **MORA.***)* You know what, FINE. She can't do anything about any of it anyway because she's IN JAIL.

MORA. She's gonna be SO MAD and whenever she gets outta jail, she's gonna yell at you and you're both gonna be so sorry—

ILLY. She's never gonna get outta jail because she's a MURDERER and an ARSONIST!

MORA. She's a WHITE LADY! She'll probably just get COMMUNITY SERVICE!

ILLY. She's not gonna DO that community service because she's CRAZY and an ADDICT and then she'll land back IN JAIL.

MORA. Well she's still gonna hate your FACE once I tell her WHAT YOU TWO ARE DOING!

> *(***ILLY*** tries to hit* **MORA** *in the head again but* **MORA** *grabs the other end of the pillow and they tug-o-war.)*

ILLY. So WHAT if she hates us! Mom and I already have a STRAINED RELATIONSHIP!

MORA. She can still be SO mad at you and you can still be SO SORRY.

ILLY. FINE! SEE IF WE CARE.

MORA. FINE!

NEEL. FINE!

ILLY & MORA. SHUT UP, NEEL.

NEEL. FINE!

MORA. FINE!

ILLY. FINE!

NEEL. FINE!!!!

ILLY. FINE!!!!!!

MORA. FINE!!!!!!

ILLY & MORA. FINE!!!!!!

> *(The pillow rips and feathers fly everywhere. They all shut up for a minute, huffing and puffing, as the feathers fall around them.)*

ILLY. Mora...

MORA. WHAT.

ILLY. What we actually wanted to tell you was—

MORA. There's more??!!

> *(**ILLY** grunts. She gets out a ukulele and starts strumming.)*

ILLY. *(Sings.)*
I, I BOUGHT THE SKY.
I BOUGHT A PART OF THE SKY
AND NOW IT'S MINE.
I, I BOUGHT THE SKY
AND ON MY PART OF THE SKY
I'LL MAKE A HOME

I'LL REHABILITATE
THIS BRAND NEW KIND OF REAL ESTATE
I'LL BRING ALONG MY BEAU
WHO HAPPENS TO BE MY BRO

WOAH

WOAH

WOAH

ILLY & NEEL. *(Sing.* **NEEL** *is tone-deaf.)*
I/SHE, I/SHE BOUGHT THE SKY
AND WITH THAT PART OF THE SKY
WE'LL MAKE A HOME.

ILLY. *(Speaks.)* See, this is our early birthday gift to you.

MORA. ...??

ILLY. Neel and I will eventually move out and live in my sky home so we're relinquishing our rights to inherit the house. Which means this is all yours.

MORA. Wait you bought the...? You mean that thing that billionaires are doing?

ILLY. Yeah—well with the money I got from the Carnegie Musicians' Award and the Trenton Ideas Award and the VanGuard Council Fellowship, and with the bump in my salaries for being principal violist in two Symphonies, and with my solo music channel on YouTube hitting twenty million views and—

> **(NEEL** *clears his throat like "maybe now is not the time to recap your achievements.")*

Basically I made enough! And I'm gonna be the youngest person to join the first wave of the human-to-sky migration. You can actually see my sky from the treehouse!

> **(MORA** *grabs some of the thrown pillows from the couch.)*

> *(She is about to exit and then turns around.)*

MORA. Neel. You're tone-deaf.

> *(She exits.)*

ILLY. I told you we should've led with the song.

NEEL. Why...would she say I was tone-deaf? I'm not tone-deaf.

> (**ILLY** *laughs. Then she realizes* **NEEL** *is not laughing.*)

I'm not. Tone-deaf. Right?

> (*A weird tension.*)

Scene iv

(**MORA** *enters the yard, with the cushions from the couch.*)

(**CAM THE SNOWMAN** *is still there.*)

(*Maybe his lines are all from distant conversations.*)

CAM THE SNOWMAN. What's shakin', bacon?

(**MORA** *throws the pillows on the floor, collapses onto them and screams into the pillows.*)

What's the stress, little mess?

MORA. Dad, did you know Illy and Neel were "together"?

CAM THE SNOWMAN. You three will always be together. [**MORA.** Oh god here we go.] That's why we decided not to tell you what countries you're adopted from, so that even if you're all different, you can all feel like you're the same. [**MORA.** Yeah, yeah, yeah.] Your origins are right here. You're from us. The Whistler family.

(**MORA** *tries to throw a pillow to shut him up but misses.*)

MORA. Damn I can't win anything today.

CAM THE SNOWMAN. You can do whatever you put your mind to, sweetie. I know you think you're a disaster but you always land on your feet.

(**MORA** *looks to* **CAM**, *a little touched. She tries to curl up next to him, but he's ice cold and she shivers.*)

You know when I feel shut out in the cold from the students I teach, I stand up in the front of the room, make myself really big, and say, "Attention, please."

MORA. "Attention, please."

*(A spotlight comes on **MORA**.)*

Oh. A spotlight, just for me. This feels nice.

Scene v

(**ILLY** *and* **NEEL**, *sitting in the treehouse again.*)

(**ILLY** *is pointing at the sky again.*)

ILLY. —And we could put the kitchen there.
And there could be a guest bathroom off the kitchen—
People always have guest bathrooms next to kitchens—

> (*She notices* **NEEL** *is not listening and takes
> out one of his earbuds.*)

Are you listening to yourself sing again?

NEEL. How would you feel if you spent twenty-eight years
not knowing this essential thing about you?

ILLY. Honestly you being tone-deaf is not, like, top five
traits about you.

NEEL. But does it make top twenty?

ILLY. If you have around twenty traits, it would be number
twenty.

NEEL. You don't think I have more than twenty traits??

ILLY. I've never counted how many traits a person has
before???

NEEL. Look, I know this may seem like it's not a huge deal
to you, but now that I know I'm tone-deaf, I might not
be Filipinx.

ILLY. Huh?

NEEL. So I know our Whistler Sibling Pact Number
Two is we don't try to guess what country we might
be adopted from so we could all proudly be Asian
adoptees parentheses country unknown until all of our
closed adoption information becomes accessible and
we go on a journey to look for each of our birth mothers
together—but I'm sorry, I just have always thought I

was Filipinx [**ILLY**. Are you sure that "x" is...?] because Filipinx people are good at singing and I thought that being really good at singing was my defining trait! But now that I'm tone-deaf, who knows what I am!!

ILLY. Where did you get the idea that being a good singer is a uniquely Filipino trait?

NEEL. Because all the famous Asian American—oops, I mean—all the famous AAPI singers are Filipinx! Bruno Mars, H.E.R., Olivia Rodrigo, Imelda Marcos—

ILLY. Imelda Marcos???

NEEL. She sings "Here Lies Love."

ILLY. ...Okay I'm sure there are people from the Philippines who are tone-deaf, and you honestly probably aren't from the Philippines because you don't loooooOOoooooo0Oo0000ooo—um, I mean, statistically speaking, it is most likely that we're from China, Korea, or Vietnam. But just two more years, Neel, and my adoption info is finally released and we find out exactly who we ethnically are—all three of us!

NEEL. You think Mora will still want to go on the journey with us after that? She seemed pretty upset...

ILLY. We made a Pact. And that was just another Mora tantrum, like that time at Wawa with the bagels. She's gonna text me tomorrow asking me to reschedule the plumber to fix the fridge's ice maker even though it's her responsibility since she broke it after she got dumped by Figgy or Twiggy or whatever that person's name was.

NEEL. No, that was after she got dumped by girl Dawn.

ILLY. Oh, I liked girl Dawn! Way better than boy Don. Although boy Don was one of the best singers I've ever—

(**NEEL** *puts his head in his hands in despair.*)

Oh no sorry I didn't mean to—!

NEEL. Isn't it just insane that I had to learn something crucial about myself from someone else? Like, what else am I wrong about? Am I not twenty-eight? Is my favorite food not banana ice cream? Do I even have arms? Illy—could you list all my traits for me? Just off the top of your head. What you can think of? Right now. List them, please, Illy, please, please, please, pretty Illy, pretty please, pretty, pretty—

ILLY. Ugh, fine! Okay, your traits. Um...
You're really sweet...and goofy...and genuine...
You definitely have arms and they're really, really great—
As is your butt! You have a good butt.
You're really good at video games.
You're an HR...assistant?

(**NEEL** *nods proudly.*)

You're kind of OCD—

NEEL. Wait, really?

ILLY. I mean, maybe not literally, but you've just always been a little...obsessive?

NEEL. Like when?

ILLY. Like...now?

(**NEEL** *starts to climb down the tree.*)

I'm sorry, I didn't think that would be a surprise to you!

NEEL. You don't understand. You know who you are. You're an accomplished musician and you're only twenty-five. Mora knows who she is. She's a disaster. I don't even know if I'm a disaster!

ILLY. What?!

NEEL. I guess...I've only known myself in the context of... well, you. You're the only real relationship I've ever had outside of my family—except that you are also my family. I... I think I have to go.

ILLY. What?!

NEEL. I have to go do something on my own. Figure out who I am.

ILLY. No, I can't hear you! I haven't been able to hear you since you started climbing down!

NEEL. I HAVE TO GO ON A—HOLD ON!

(**NEEL** *finds a song on his phone.*)

I HAVE TO GO ON A ...

(**NEEL** *plays a journey song.** *He sings along but he is still tone-deaf.*)

ILLY. I DON'T GET IT!

NEEL. JOURNEY!!! TONE-DEAF NEEL IS TAKING A TONE-DEAF JOURNEY TO FIND WHAT ELSE HE'S GOT GOING ON!

(**NEEL** *exits in a huff.*)

ILLY. Wait, Neel! Neel, where are you going? Neel?

(*Something drops on* **ILLY***'s head and she screams.*)

(*She examines the thing that dropped.*)

(*It is a dead bird.*)

(*She looks to the sky and wonders where it came from.*)

---

*A license to produce *Regretfully, So the Birds Are* does not include a performance license for any third-party or copyrighted music. Licensees should create an original composition or use music in the public domain. For further information, please see the Music and Third-Party Materials Use Note on page iii.

Scene vi

(A visiting room. **MORA** *and* **ELINORE** *sit across from each other.)*

MORA. Mom.
Neel and Illy...are having.
.... An affair.

ELINORE. That...can't be true.

MORA. I know, I couldn't believe it either but—

ELINORE. They can't have an affair. Neither of them is married.

MORA. But you can have an affair if—

ELINORE. I know I can but I'm married. You know who had affairs?

MORA. Dad?

ELINORE. I'm Mom.

MORA. Oh my god, are you listening to me?? Illy and Neel are having a—a—a thing.

ELINORE. Is it a salad spinner? I always wanted a salad spinner but every time I look at the price I think to myself, "My colander is good enough."

MORA. *(Hand out.)* All right. Hand 'em over.

ELINORE. Well I don't have my colander on me now.

MORA. The Vicodin. Or whatever drug you somehow managed to sneak in here.

ELINORE. Oh sweetie I'm not high again, I'm just in jail.

MORA. Then why aren't you upset that your children are romantically involved with each other?

ELINORE. It means we're a happy family.

MORA. You incinerated our dad.

ELINORE. Yes, and now I'm happy. And how's my Mora doing?

MORA. Not great to be honest!!

ELINORE. Aww, does Mora want a little pat-pat?

MORA. Mom...

ELINORE. I know you do...

> (**MORA** *relents and puts her head on the table.*
> **ELINORE** *strokes her hair.*)

There you go. Mora. My Mora, my oldest, first, miracle child of mine, born just for me. You're turning thirty tomorrow, right? Wow. Thirty. I thought by thirty you'd have a spouse and a house—oh, I rhymed!—and I thought you'd have a job and health insurance and a savings account and a retirement plan and a good set of life skills and a decent amount of sense in that pretty little head of yours, and you have none of those things! Because my Mora doesn't go down the path already traveled. No, my Mora makes all the wrong choices and still comes out the other end a strong, independent woman. You're a lot like me in that way, you know.

MORA. Okay, bye.

> (**ELINORE** *grabs onto* **MORA**'s *wrist.*)

ELINORE. No Mora don't go, please, please, please, pretty Mora, pretty please, pretty, pretty—

MORA. Don't "pretty, pretty" me—

ELINORE. I want to give you a present! I thought for your thirtieth, it would be nice to give you your adoption information. I know you three have your Pact about waiting to find out but it can be our special little secret. Especially because I don't want to remind the other two that I don't like them as much.

MORA. Wow... Mom, that would... *(Takes a deep breath.)* Oh my god, I'm about to find out where I'm really from—

ELINORE. But the thing you need to know is that I really wanted to keep out of your adoption business because I didn't want to care where you came from or how you got to me, I just wanted you for you, Mora, my beautiful, independent girl. So I don't remember what country you're from but I—

MORA. EXCUSE ME?

ELINORE. There was just so much going on—this was during PEAK Vicodin-popping Mommy Elinore phase, you know? And obviously I sautéed your father before I could ask him to remind me, which was poor planning on my part, I know—But we did keep your adoption file and it is taped under the second drawer of his filing cabinet in a purple envelope, because I know that's your favorite color—

MORA. You mean the filing cabinet in the office you burned. When you burned Dad. In his office.

ELINORE. But the filing cabinet didn't burn, did it? That thing was very sturdy.

MORA. It did.

ELINORE. Huh. Woops.

MORA. You really can't remember the ONE WORD that could identify my heritage? Listen, I cut you a lot of slack for all the shit you've been through but this is not forgetting when the plumber is coming to fix the fridge's ice maker—I forgot to tell Illy when the plumber is coming to fix the fridge's ice maker—this is about my LIFE SO GET IT THE FUCK TOGETHER OR—

ELINORE. Okay! Okay. I...DO remember that the country you're from starts with a C. I remember that really, really clearly.

MORA. ...So...China?

ELINORE. I would remember if it was China, China is very famous.

MORA. Cambodia…?

ELINORE. Are there others? What about Croatia?

MORA. All those years married to an Asian History professor…

ELINORE. But not a very good one according to RateMyProfessor.com.

Well. Happy early Birthday, Mora. My baby made just for me. All the way from Cambodega.

MORA. CAMBODIA. Cambodia. Oh my god I'm from Cambodia… I'm…Cambodian…

Scene vii

(**CAM THE SNOWMAN** *is standing in the yard as before.*)

(**NEEL** *enters with a box of stuff, which is mostly video games. He takes video games out of the box one by one to examine if they give him joy. With every "joy" he puts it back in the box.*)

NEEL. Joy. Joy. Joy. No jo... (*Changes his mind.*) Joy! Joy—

(**MORA** *walks into the yard to grab a couch cushion.*)

Hey, Mora. Joy—

MORA. (*As she exits with the cushion.*) Not talking to you!!

NEEL. Okay! Joy. Joy. Joy—

CAM THE SNOWMAN. What's up, buttercup?

NEEL. Dad, I'm gonna go on a journey to find myself but according to the Spark Joy lady, it has to start with a cleanse. I was gonna cleanse myself of these video games. But...they taught me so much. Like Duck Hunt taught me how to hunt ducks. And Mario Kart taught me about Italian brotherhood.

MORA. (*From offstage.*) Where's the blowtorch??

NEEL. Under the kitchen sink!

MORA. (*From offstage.*) Thanks!

(**MORA** *continues to call from offstage throughout the line below.*)

NEEL. (*To* **MORA**.) You're welcome! (*To himself.*) Come to think of it, Luigi is a supportive brother, like me. Maybe I should try to be, like, the Asian Luigi. [**MORA**. Wait, How do you turn this thing on?] Wait a minute.

If Luigi was made in Japan, is Luigi the Asian Luigi? But isn't Luigi [**MORA**. Neel? How do you turn it— WAHH!!] canonically Italian? Is Luigi Japanese Italian? Italian Japanese? [**MORA**. I figured it out!!] Oh my god is Luigi mixed race?? What do you think, Dad?

CAM THE SNOWMAN. I think it's all gonna be okay, Neel.

NEEL. Thanks...

> (**MORA** *walks out and grabs another pillow.*)

Mora, what are you doing?

MORA. Making a neck pillow. What are you doing?

NEEL. Preparing to go on a journey.

MORA. (*As she's exiting.*) Where?

NEEL. ...Huh. I didn't even think of that. Where should I go, Dad?? Where does one go on a tone-deaf journey?

CAM THE SNOWMAN. You know I've always wanted to take a family trip to Asia. I've always wanted to meet the Asian people in their true communities.

NEEL. I should go somewhere famous for their music! Maybe the people there can help me overcome my tone-deafness. I know! I'll head to the heart of country music: Nebraska.

> (**NEEL** *starts exiting with his video games.*)

> (**MORA** *comes out with a charred part of the cushion vaguely resembling a neck pillow.*)

I figured out where I'm going: Nebraska!

MORA. Why?

NEEL. (*As he's exiting.*) To find myself!

MORA. Oh, that's genius. I'll tell Illy and Neel that I'm going to Cambodia to find myself. It's believable because my

life is a disaster. I'm not gonna tell them I'm going to go
find my birth mother so they think I'm still maintaining
our Pact, but also because they kept a secret from me
and now I get to keep a secret from them.

I've got this great plan to find my birth mother!
I'm gonna walk up to every person in Cambodia.
And I'm gonna say,
"Hi. I'm sorry to interrupt your day.
But I was wondering.
Did you give up a baby girl for adoption thirty years ago?
With a scar on the side of her neck?"
And I'll show them the scar on my neck.
And if they say "No."
I will say,
"Are you sure? I'm not a cop so you don't have to lie to me."
And if they still say, "No."
I will say,
"Okay. Thank you for your time."
And if they say "Yes."
I will say,
"Oh. That's wonderful. I think I'm that baby girl thirty
years later."
And then we'll play it by ear from there. Doesn't that
sound great, Dad?

CAM THE SNOWMAN. Do you know what language they
speak in Cambodia?

MORA & CAM THE SNOWMAN. The language native to
the country and the language of the country that
colonized them.

CAM THE SNOWMAN. So in Cambodia they speak Khmer
and—

MORA. Sorry I don't have time to learn about whatever
that is. My neck pillow for my journey is complete!
I think I'm ready to go then. Bye, Dad! Bye, bye
America! I'll see you soon. Ahem. Attention, please!

(A spotlight on **MORA.***)*

*(***NEEL*** comes back on with a suitcase and sees* **MORA.***)*

MORA. I'm off to Cambodia, population: 15 million and growing.

NEEL. Cool. Attention, please!

(A spotlight on **NEEL.***)*

I'm off to Nebraska, population: 1.9 million and growing.

MORA. 25% of the population of Cambodia was killed by the reign of Pol Pot.

NEEL. 87.7% of the population of Nebraska is white.

MORA. I'm going to Cambodia to "find myself"! *(Winks.)*

NEEL. I'm going to Nebraska to find myself!

MORA. *(To* **NEEL.***)* Stop copying me!

NEEL. Well you're copying me by going to find yourself.

MORA.	**NEEL.**
You can't just take my thing—you always do this! You copy the things that Illy or I are interested in because you don't have a personality to find the things you are interested in on your own—	Plus you make literally everything about yourself all the time—why do you get to have the extra attention? Also my spotlight is way smaller than yours even though I'm way taller—
ILLY!	ILLY!

(Lights on **ILLY** *who is in her tree.)*

ILLY. ...Hm?

MORA.

I'm going on a journey to find myself in Cambodia

And he's trying to copy me.

Who do you think is right?

NEEL.

I'm going on a journey to find myself in Nebraska

And she's trying to copy me.

Who do you think is right?

ILLY. You're *both* going on journeys??

MORA & NEEL.

Yeah, so I'm gonna be hard to reach for a while— you know how travel is.

Miss you! Love you! I'll send you a postcard once I get there!

Bye bye!

ILLY.

So I'm supposed to take care of Mom and the house and everything alone? I mean I guess I'm basically doing that now but it would help if either of you tried to—

Wait!

(*Spotlights go off on* **MORA** *and* **NEEL** *and they exit.*)

(**ILLY** *looks around confused and shocked about what just happened.*)

(*Her breath starts to get fast, as if she might panic or cry. She takes a deep breath and looks at the sky.*)

ILLY. That's mine. That's my sky. A sky just for me.

(*She starts pointing at the clouds.*)

And you are mine.
And you are mine.
And you are—

(**A BIRD** *crashes into* **ILLY.**)

*(Each of **A BIRD**'s line of text should move rapidly, like they're one word, but the time in between each line of text could be as long or as short as needed.)*

A BIRD. Oh oh oh
I'm
So so so
Sorry ahhh sorry!

ILLY. That's okay. I'm glad you're alive. Lately I've been getting some dead ones...

A BIRD. It's true it's true
We die we die
A lot a lot a lot of us
Air air air
Before
Clear and clear and
But now poof poof
Cough cough

ILLY. Is there particularly bad air quality in this neighborhood? Because if there is, I really need to get some money back.

A BIRD. What you?
A You? A You? A You?

ILLY. I'm Illy and I actually bought that part of the sky so if you have any concerns about it I'd—

A BIRD. Buy?
Buy sky?
But
Sky is
Sky is
Free free

ILLY. Oh it definitely wasn't free.

A BIRD. Illy Illy
No, no, no buy sky
Sky is Sky is

ILLY. I know, this is the sky, and that part of it is mine.

A BIRD. No no no

ILLY. Yes yes yes!

A BIRD. Suspect.
Suspect Illy
Illy suspect
Suss
Peck

> (**A BIRD** *pecks* **ILLY** *in the shoulder.*)

ILLY. Ow!

A BIRD. No my my my!
No buy no buy!
Goodbye!

> (**A BIRD** *flies away.*)

> (**ILLY** *tries to shake off the feathers on her from* **A BIRD.***)*

> (*She realizes some of them are covered in blood.*)

Scene viii

(**CAM THE SNOWMAN** *is still there in the yard.*)

CAM THE SNOWMAN. More fun facts:

Pol Pot fell in love with his first wife when he saw they shared the same political values.

Pol Pot divorced his first wife when she started having chronic schizophrenia and would tell him that he was going to be assassinated.

Pol Pot fell in love with his second wife because she didn't think he was a bad guy.

Cam Whistler fell in love with Asia when he saw *Enter the Dragon* as a teenager at Dani Dee's sweet sixteenth birthday party.

Cam Whistler fell in love with his wife when he saw how well she could use chopsticks at the sushi restaurant they went to on their sixteenth date.

Cam Whistler fell in love with his first mistress when she sighed.

Cam Whistler fell in love with his second mistress when she raised her hand.

What's a good love song?

(*He whistles a tune.*)

Cam Whistler was tone-deaf but nobody knew because he never sang.

(*Another bird drops dead from the sky.*)

ACT TWO: Dramatic Journey

Scene i

(In darkness, there is the sound of many journeys.)

(There is also the sound of many birds squawking and chattering.)

(Perhaps in the cacophony, we hear a phone ringing.)

(When lights are up, we are both at home and very far from home.)

*(**MORA** and **ILLY**, far away, and on their phones, are in mid-conversation.)*

ILLY. Why didn't you ever tell me that you were trying to let Neel live his whole life believing he wasn't tone-deaf?

MORA. Why didn't you ever tell me you and Neel were together?

ILLY. Well we're not together right now.

MORA. Please don't tell me you broke up. I can't have exes as siblings. That's even more insane than having lovers as siblings.

ILLY. What if you dated and broke up with a guy and then his sister? You would then still have exes as siblings and that seems like a highly possible situation for you.

MORA. I go on a date with a set of twins ONCE and I never stop hearing about it, but meanwhile, my brother and my sister are having an affair and I'm still the disaster—

ILLY. We're not having an affair, neither of us—

MORA. ARE MARRIED, I GOT IT, JESUS!!

ILLY. I honestly don't even know what we're having anymore...

MORA. ...Do you...want to...talk...about it...?

ILLY. Do you want to talk about it?

MORA. I'm trying to be a good sister but everything is hard.

ILLY. Yeah why do you think I'm dating Neel?

MORA. Are you telling me it is easy to date your brother?

ILLY. It's easy dating someone who already knows your shit and is cool with your shit because it's very similar and sometimes identical to his shit.

MORA. I would NEVER date either of you.

ILLY. Well you're also not attracted to either of us—

MORA. *(Convulsing.)* AH AH AH.

ILLY. It's okay we can talk about something else—

MORA. Illy, you could have any guy out there, so WHY are you choosing Neel?? Like I'll put aside the brother thing for two seconds—this is a guy who is currently on his way to Nebraska because he thinks it's Nashville.

ILLY. I dunno, it doesn't make sense to me either half the time, but he makes me laugh and he's so cute when he's stupid and...he's always shown up. Like every concert, every award ceremony, graduation... [**MORA.** I really did try to be at your—] And I get it, Mom had her episodes and you had things going on...but it's just nice to feel like someone will always be there.

MORA. But didn't Dad show up to a lot of your recitals—

ILLY. Um, what? Who?

MORA. Okay I know we made that Pact but we kinda have to talk about Dad sometimes, no? I know what he did was shitty, but he was still—

ILLY. I'm sorry, I don't know who you're talking about. Are you in Cambodia?

MORA. I'm in a layover in Guangzhou, China. Did you know some people in China do karaoke at funerals? I learned that from the China travel video on the plane.

ILLY. Since you're in China, maybe you'll run into your birth mom.

MORA. Why would you say that right now, nothing anyone is doing has anything to do with birth moms right now, that's so weird.

ILLY. It's highly likely you're Chinese. Right? Because you kinda looooooooooooo0000oo000ooooooo00oooo oooOOO—I mean statistically-speaking—

MORA. I look Chinese?

ILLY. That's so racist, I would never ever say that.

MORA. I don't think it's racist for us to say we look Chinese.

ILLY. But, Mora, we're not, like…really Asian—

MORA. Are you still not making friends with the other AAPI—oops, I mean AANHPI people in your orchestra?

ILLY. AANHPI? What does the NH stand for?

MORA. New Hampshire.

ILLY. You're lying.

MORA. You would know if you made more AANHPI friends. I don't know why you don't, you're the most Asian person out there with the whole overachieving music genius thing.

ILLY. That's not what makes someone Asian, those are just stereotypes and stereotypes are racist. Like Neel thought he was Filipino because he thinks Filipinos are good at singing—

MORA. Ohhh yeahhh they are!

ILLY. No, Mora, that's a stereotype—

MORA. But all the famous AANHPI singers are Filipinx.

ILLY. What is with this x, isn't that just for Latinx people? [**MORA.** Latine.] Also—Neel is, like, definitely not Filipino, right?

MORA. I dunno, Illy, we could be anything. Neel could be Filipino... I could be...Cambodian.

ILLY. But you don't looooooo—Wait are you going to Cambodia because you think you're Cambodian?

MORA. No! Just. Musing. 'Cause. I'm gonna. Be there. And stuff.

ILLY. Right, right, you're all finding yourselves without me like I'm not enough for you or something.

MORA. Aww Illy... Play your moody violin for me? I love it when you play your moody violin.

ILLY. IT'S A VIOLA and you're 8000 miles away. It won't be the same.

MORA. Well, I'll press my body up against this window that looks out on the tarmac. And every time I feel vibrations from the jets, I'll pretend like it's the strings on your viola. And with every sensation, I'll think about how you've carried this family, and how cool it is that you're joining the human-to-sky migration, and how hurt you feel to have your brother and sister abandon you, even though I also feel—but it doesn't matter what I feel! Because this is for you to know that someone is out there who is listening to you with her whole body— ew, there's something sticky on this window.

ILLY. Mora... I'm... I'm sorry we didn't—

MORA. This is about you.

ILLY. Any requests?

MORA. Can you make something up for me?

ILLY. Do you have $5,000? That's my minimum for viola commissions.

MORA. I don't get a family discount?!

ILLY. Ukulele is only $100, and I can put it on your tab.

MORA. Fine.

> (**ILLY** *blows a raspberry into the phone and* **MORA** *blows one back.* **ILLY** *thinks a little on what to make up for her sister. Then she picks up her ukulele. She sings a little ditty like:*)

ILLY. *(Sings.)*
THE DAISY WILL WILT
AND THE SNOW WILL MELT
AND WE'LL ALL GO HOME
TO THE GROUND
TO THE GROUND
WE'LL ALL GO HOME TO THE GROUND

> (**ILLY** *continues strumming or singing on "dahs" below.*)

> (**MORA** *presses her body up against the airport window. She is sort of listening to her sister play but she also starts to think about how she needs to look up laundry customs in Cambodia.*)

> (**SREY** *enters.*)

> (*She watches* **MORA** *pressed up against the window.*)

> (**MORA** *turns around, sees* **SREY**, *and yelps a little in surprise.*)

> (*Then* **MORA** *stares at* **SREY**, *who stares back.*)

MORA. Excuse me, are you also getting on this flight to Cambodia? Are you from Cambodia?

(**SREY** *nods.*)

Okay, I have this thing that I wanna ask every person in Cambodia...and, um, well, I'll just try it out and...

Hi.
I'm sorry to interrupt your day.
But I was wondering.
Um. Did you, um.
Give up a baby girl for adoption thirty years ago?
With a scar on the side of her neck?

(**MORA** *shows* **SREY** *her scar.*)

Oh, wait do you even speak—?

SREY. Yes.

MORA. Are you saying yes, like, you speak English, or yes you did give up a baby girl...?

SREY. Yes. Yes.

MORA. Oh. OH! Well... That's wonderful. I mean—it might not have been wonderful! It might have been sad! But... I think... I think I might be that baby girl... thirty years later.

(**SREY** *hugs* **MORA**.)

(**ILLY** *stops playing.*)

ILLY. I just made that up for you, Mora. Do you like it?

(**ILLY** *looks into the space and hears the silence.*)

Happy Thirtieth Birthday, Mora.

(*A very large screech from the sky.*)

Scene ii

(Nebraska. **NEEL** *arrives with his suitcase, alone.)*

NEEL. I finally made it! Nebraska!

(He stands waiting for something to happen.)

(But nothing happens. I mean, this is Nebraska.)

It's so flat.

(A **COWMAN** *slowly enters. He wears a cowboy hat deep on his head so you can't see his eyes. He's got that kinda swagger that makes you wonder whether a knee is a sexual organ.)*

*(***NEEL** *waves at him.)*

Excuse me, sir! Mr. Cowboy!

COWMAN. I'm a cowMAN, son.

NEEL. Sorry. Do you know where the country music people hang out?

COWMAN. Do you want to lean up against me like I'm a big oak tree?

NEEL. Um... you know what, sure. Why not?

*(***NEEL** *sits on the floor and leans his back on the* **COWMAN**'s *legs.)*

Do you sing country music?

COWMAN. That's a stereotype.

NEEL. ...Noted...

COWMAN. Do you want to tell me about your daddy issues?

NEEL. Oh, I don't have issues with my dad. I just have this weird thing where my sisters and I made a Pact not to talk about him because our mom revealed to us only after she burned him that he was kind of a bad person, but I think about him all the time because he was the only consistent man in my life so he was kind of a role model for me, which makes me scared that I'm gonna turn out to be just like him, but then sometimes I think he couldn't possibly have been the man my mom said he was because he was kind of a good dad to me and a good dad can't be a bad person, but then that makes me scared I'm already the kind of bad person he was, and then on top of all that I think his last words to me were "We're out of ranch," so now every time I see ranch I feel...really sad. But those aren't really daddy issues, they're more like daddy volumes.

(He laughs at the joke he made.)

Daddy volumes...

*(***NEEL*** continues to laugh at his own joke looking to the* ***COWMAN*** *to see if he'll laugh with him but* ***COWMAN*** *doesn't budge.* ***NEEL*** *keeps laughing but then the laughs start to sound like violent sobs.)*

*(***COWMAN*** *takes off his hat and hands it to* ***NEEL.*** *We should never be able to see the* ***COWMAN***'s *face so he should be facing upstage, or perhaps underneath his hat there is another hat.)*

*(***NEEL*** *takes the hat and hides his face and then screams into the hat.)*

(He hands the hat back to the ***COWMAN.***)*

Thank you.

(A little bird chirps in the sky.)

(**NEEL** *looks up.*)

Wow. The sky is so…big here. I swear it's bigger here than in New Jersey. Isn't that weird? Even though the sky is supposed to be the same everywhere.

COWMAN. Sky is the freest thing in this stratosphere.

(*The* **COWMAN** *exits, whistling.*)

NEEL. Yeah, sky is the freest thing in the…

OH.

Scene iii

> *(A visiting room again.* **ILLY** *and* **ELINORE** *sit across from each other.)*

ELINORE. What's...wrong...?

ILLY. You called me.

ELINORE. —with your face? Did you always have this resting bitch face?

> *(***ILLY*** *gets up to leave.)*

No Illy don't go, please, please, please, pretty Illy, pretty please, pretty, pretty—

ILLY. You told me on the phone this was an emergency!

ELINORE. Yes, it is! Illy: you may not be my best-liked but you are objectively the most responsible. Honestly you're the most responsible person I know—although I hear you're dating Neel which makes me question that a little—

ILLY. Mora told you?!

ELINORE. Don't be mad at her. She only gets so many wins in her life. Now, Illy, I'm not in any position to tell you who to date, considering my own choices were not so great—oh, I rhymed!—but if you're going to be with Neel I'm just begging you not to birth children with him because you really don't want to pass along whatever he's got in his DNA. *(Whispers.)* He's not very bright.

ILLY. I kinda like that about him, okay!

ELINORE. So where did you and Neel meet?

ILLY. Mom!

ELINORE. Just pretend like I don't know everything there is to know about him, make up some fun story—I've never gotten to do this kind of girl talk with you.

ILLY. I'm not gonna sit here and pretend to live in some alternate reality where—

ELINORE. Oh you should from time to time, it can be so relaxing—and maybe it could help you chill out a little, sweetie, you're a little *(She mimes a tight screw.)*. You weren't always like this, you know—remember when you were a tiny tot and you'd run around hitting your brother, I mean, your boyfriend in the head with the little toy violin that your father got you?

ILLY. Didn't you get me that toy violin?

ELINORE. No your father, may he rest in hell, really wanted to encourage the arts in you three, even though I always say arts is farts without the f. And you were the only one who took to it, which he got so excited about because he was always a big fan of Grimaldi [**ILLY**. Vivaldi] and Chinaman [**ILLY**. Tchaikovsky] and he took you to all those, those... what are they called those, those... those things... you do them, you do them all the time now, on the stage, with all the music...

ILLY. You mean concerts?

ELINORE. Concerts! Yes, I knew that I... but you two would go off to those and then come back and make up little songs—

ILLY. Did you actually have something to tell me?

ELINORE. Oh YES! This is actually really important—as I was saying—Illy: you may not be my best-liked but you are objectively the most—

ILLY. Fast forward, please.

ELINORE. You have to hide the valuables. They're coming. I heard them. I heard them at their meetings—their little council meetings—and they are very angry, so angry—they think that we're killing them—and they're holding all these funerals—and singing karaoke at the funerals—and they're very upset and they're coming for us, specifically—

ILLY. Who? Who's coming?

ELINORE. Them! You know the little, the little, the little cheep cheep cheep—oh what are they called—the little cheep cheep cheep squawk squawk squawk—

ILLY. Birds? I think they're just confused—like one crashed into me and couldn't understand that I bought—

ELINORE. They've gotten to you already! Oh no, oh dear. They're coming for you—they're coming for the house— are they coming for me next—or Mora! What if they come for Mora next! Oh, Illy, Illy, we have to protect her, please protect my baby—

ILLY. She's gonna be fine! She's all the way in Cambodia.

ELINORE. Mora went to Cambodia? Oh shit.

ILLY. What's wrong with her going to Cambodia?

ELINORE. Illy, you know how everybody makes mistakes?

(Birds chatter.)

Scene iv

SREY. Attention, please.

*(Spotlight on **SREY**, alone onstage.)*

Once, there was a young girl who had two great loves.
The first was the Chinese Opera.
She had never seen it live.
But she had a record she played over and over.
Her other great love was the boy who lived next door.
Every sunset, they would meet by a rock that looked like a fox.
Here she would practice the songs and dances for him.

But one day.
The girl came to the rock.
And waited.
And waited.
And it grew very dark but he did not come.
And something deep within her knew something was wrong.
So she ran. Fast.
Far, far away from their village, their home.
And as she arrived in the new city she thought, "I am alone."

But, as she would discover in a few weeks, she wasn't entirely alone.
In the city, a ticket to the opera was very expensive.
So she worked and she worked.
But soon she needed to eat for two.
She would press her ear against the outer wall of the theatre.
"So close, and yet so far."

Then one day.
A stranger passing by whispered an address in her ear.

SREY. And when she followed the address, she found an agency offering money
In exchange for her soon-to-be child
All that remained of the boy she loves.
How cruel a world it is where only one love is allowed.

Before relinquishing her child, she carved a small scratch on her neck.
So that should they ever meet again she would recognize her daughter.

Thirty years later.
This woman, no longer so young, is in an airport in Guangzhou, China,
Where she has just performed her signature role at the Guangzhou Opera House.
As this Opera Performer searches for her gate, she doesn't have the faintest idea
That her daughter might be on a layover in Guangzhou, China, searching for her.

The Opera Performer passes by a thirty-year-old woman, with her body pressed up against the window.
The Opera Performer stops and stares at this strange thirty-year-old.
Something is drawing her in.
So she steps closer
And closer
The thirty-year-old pressed against the window tilts her head, revealing a mark upon her neck.
An old scar from thirty years ago.
The Opera Performer is about to take another step when she remembers:
"Oh dear!"
Her boarding time is near.
So the Opera Performer turns around
And runs off to her gate...
	...

So close, and yet so far.

...

And then there was another woman, also in this airport—
The Opera Performer's Biggest Fan, in fact—
Who was following this Opera Performer
And happened to be just at the right place, at the right time
To witness this miracle almost happen... and then not...

And then this other woman thinks to herself:
What if I chose to live in a world in which this miracle does occur...?
I do love a good story.
(This other woman is me. In case that wasn't clear.)

Scene v

(**ILLY** *sitting in the treehouse.*)

(*Meanwhile* **A BIRD** *from before has landed on a tree branch and seems to be "watching" her.*)

(**ILLY** *dials a number. We hear it go straight to voicemail.*)

(*"You've reached Neel! Leave a message at the... at the... wait how do I know when the bee– BEEP."*)

ILLY. Neel I really need you to call me back because Mom's in a situation and Mora's in a situation and UGH I just remembered I have to reschedule the plumber again to fix the fridge's ice maker!

(*Hangs up.*)

(*A panic starts to creep in.*)

(*She looks to the sky, and takes a deep breath.*)

That's mine. That's my sky. A sky just for me.

(*She starts pointing at the clouds.*)

And you are mine
And you are mine
And—

(*Then the tree starts rustling.*)

(**NEEL** *climbs up the tree.*)

NEEL. Illy! I'm back! I'm sorry I left but I had a really—

(**ILLY** *grabs him and kisses him.*)

(*He very gently removes himself from her.*)

Okay I really wanna get back to this but I kinda planned this big speech, so could I just...?

Ahem.

Illy, I'm sorry I left but I had a really productive journey and I had to come back as soon as possible to tell you something I realized: I'm an environmentalist! Remember how I majored in Environmental Studies in college? It was the only major that could be fulfilled by all the random classes I took BUT I remember going to some of the classes and thinking: I really dig this! Like I really do believe we have to protect the planet at all costs.

And... Illy... it's not right for you to buy the sky. I know all you want is a place that's yours but occupying a space where mammals aren't supposed to be really messes with the ecosystem. According to the environmentalists' subreddit, there's this weird new disease in the bird community in the greater North East, and people think it's connected to the fact that the first wave of the human-to-sky migration has begun. So I think you really need to return the sky, because the sky is the freest thing in the stratosphere.

ILLY. ...

...
No.

NEEL. No?

ILLY. Have you even listened to my voicemails? I think there's something wrong with Mom's brain so they're doing another psych eval—And have you talked to Mora since she's landed in Cambodia? I haven't been able to get a hold of her and Mom did something absolutely unhinged which is tell her—

NEEL. Maybe there's spotty Wi-Fi wherever she is. But, seriously, Illy, can you maybe agree to give back the sky, because I thought it would be great as my first post for my environmental activism vlog to show you returning the sky—

ILLY. If you think the "ENVIRONMENT" is more important than "YOUR SISTER" or "YOUR MOTHER" or "YOUR GIRLFRIEND" who is staring right at you, then you can sit here and rot in this treehouse and your rotting bones can protect the sky and the birds forever.

(**ILLY** *starts climbing down the tree.*)

(*Mumbly grumbly.*) Jesus fucking christ why couldn't we just make out instead of having him open his goddamned mouth my god—

NEEL. What did you say? Illy? ...Illy?

(**A BIRD**, *who has been on the branch this whole time, hops over to* **NEEL** *and pecks him.*)

Ow! Oh, hello!

A BIRD. Illy mate?
You Illy mate?
You a You a You?

NEEL. Me? Yeah I'm Illy's mate.

A BIRD. Suspect
Suspect Illy mate
Illy mate suspect
Peck.

(**A BIRD** *pecks* **NEEL** *again and flies away.*)

NEEL. Wow. I think I just made my first friend in the bird community.

Scene vi

(**MORA** *and* **SREY** *are sitting on an airplane together.*)

(**MORA** *still has her neck pillow around her neck.*)

SREY. This is Mora, telling me her life story.

MORA. —Then I joined my mountain climbing partner on a cross-country road trip—but halfway through he broke up with me and I broke my tibia and Illy came all the way to Utah to—

SREY. This is Mora, telling me her traits.

MORA. I'm kind of loud?
And emotional.
And…some people say I'm… and I, too, would, say I'm a—
Oh! I'm an older sister. That's important.
I mean I don't really act like one but I… I am one.

SREY. This is Mora, telling me everything she knows about Cambodia.

MORA. You know a lot of people find this surprising but Pol Pot was actually a very compelling teacher—that's what my dad said anyway—

SREY. This is Mora five months before she gets assassinated.

Mora will be assassinated because some people in Cambodia will fear she will become another dictator.

They will fear she will become another dictator because she will frequently reference Pol Pot in her speeches.

She will frequently reference Pol Pot in her speeches because Pol Pot is her main frame of reference for Cambodia.

You see, her father was not a very good Asian history professor.

SREY. I don't point this out to her, of course.
Or stop her from talking about Pol Pot.
I am a very affirming mother.

MORA. Oh my god I think I just talked at you for this
whole flight?? Sometimes I think I inherited some of
my mom's crazy—I know it's problematic to call her
crazy—she's just not well and—

SREY. My mother was also not well. Schizophrenia.

MORA. Oh wow... mine's just an opioid addict...
Oh! Today is my birthday, actually. I dunno if you
remember...?

SREY. Happy birthday.
My name is Srey,
By the way.

MORA. Oh. You rhymed.

(**SREY** *looks at* **MORA.**)

Sorry it's a thing my mom... never mind. It's so nice to
meet you, Srey.

Scene vii

(**CAM THE SNOWMAN** *is still in the yard.*)

CAM THE SNOWMAN. Less fun facts:
Cam Whistler was not a very good Asian History professor.
He loved Asia, but also believed it was full of dangerous,
evil people.
That's what his favorite movies taught him.
So when he and his wife discussed adoption, he suggested
adopting from Asia—
So he could save a child from all the dangerous, evil people.
But soon after the adoption,
He started having nightmares that his daughter would
be assassinated.
Assassinated because people feared she would become
a dictator in Asia.
These nightmares tortured him nightly.
He couldn't tell his wife about them because she was
not always well.
He couldn't tell his daughter about them because that
would be bad parenting.
So he did something he had never done before:
Research.
(The college hiring process is very flawed.)
He read all the Asian History textbooks he could find—
But only the sections on dictators.
And when he finished reading all he could find,
He turned to the next best alternative to Asian History
textbooks:
Asian people.
More specifically.
His Asian students.
More specifically.
Female Asian students.

You know a lot of people find this surprising but Pol
Pot was actually a very compelling teacher.

Scene viii

(**ELINORE** *is sitting on the cushion-less couch with an ankle monitor.*)

(**ILLY** *and* **NEEL** *are in mid-argument behind the couch.*)

ILLY.
—You wanna talk about diseases then why not start with Mom's? Do you want to take her to her follow-up appointments? Do you want to give her medicine? If you're not even interested in helping take care of the things I'm taking care of then you really aren't in any position to tell me what I'm doing with my own money—

NEEL.
—See, this study proved that the new disease in birds is about the air in the sky shifting and—

Okay that's not fair, you know hospitals make me queasy—but that has nothing to do with the fact that you are literally killing birds right now! You have so much money that you could buy a house literally anywhere else—

ELINORE.
I could have sworn this couch had more cushions...

(*A phone that happens to be next to* **ELINORE** *starts ringing. She picks it up.*)

Mora? Mora! Hello my Mora dear, can you see me?

(*Somewhere,* **MORA** *is on FaceTime.*)

MORA. Mom? I thought I called Illy?

ELINORE. Illy, can you figure out if my baby can see me?

ILLY. (*Grabs the phone.*) Mora! Where the hell have you been?! We've been trying to reach you for weeks!

MORA. I know, I'm sorry, my pocket Wi-Fi is kind of spotty.

NEEL. *(To* **ILLY.***)* I told you.

ELINORE. Can she see me? Make sure she can see me!

MORA. How is Mom home?

ILLY. We had them do another psych eval and she's not fit to stand trial—

ELINORE. I'm legally crazy now!

ILLY. She just has dementia and they let her home because it progressed really fast. They think it's a side effect from her addiction.

NEEL. Don't worry Illy's taking care of everything as usual except the innocent creatures of the earth—

ILLY. Oh my god—Neel thinks I'm a murderer just for trying to build a home—

ELINORE. Murderers do run in the family—

MORA. FAM! Can you shut up for a second because I actually have something important to tell you? First of all, I'm doing fine, thank you for asking. Cambodia's really great—Dad always talked about it like it was some underdeveloped, impoverished place, but Phnom Penh is really modern! And...on the plane ride here I met this woman...and miraculously it turned out that she's—

ELINORE. *(To* **NEEL.***)* You owe me ten bucks.

NEEL. Dammit Mora I thought this one time you wouldn't pull a Mora and have a love affair three seconds into—

MORA. THAT'S WHAT I'VE BEEN TRYING TO SAY! That Illy and Neel have been having a LOVE affair! Do you see what I mean??

(*The* **FAM** *all shrug.*)

Anyway, I'm not having a love affair. The real news is... I found my birth mother!

(Silence.)

MORA. Fam?

ILLY. Sorry, you broke up there—

ELINORE. Did you say you found your catheter?

MORA. My BIRTH MOTHER.

NEEL. WHAT?! You abandoned our Pact?!

ILLY. Mora, I really don't think that's true—

MORA. Illy, just because I don't look Cambodian—

ILLY. You're not Cambodian because you were adopted from Guangzhou, China!

ELINORE. It was the G word I couldn't remember!

NEEL. Woah, woah, how did we all know about Mora's ethnicity except me! First I'm tone-deaf—now Mora's Chinese?

ELINORE. That's why you love dumplings so much.

MORA. GUYS! I know all this, Srey is Cambodian but she is of mixed Chinese heritage and she took me to an adoption agency in Guangzhou because she felt she could be more anonymous. I checked out all her paperwork and everything, trust me. And learning about her and Cambodia and the culture and the people...it's been a lot.

> *(At this point, the following happens silently as* **MORA** *keeps talking:* **ELINORE** *tries to grab the phone closer but instead it slips out of* **ILLY**'s *hand and crashes to the floor. Everyone scrambles to get it.* **NEEL** *grabs the phone and it is clear from his reaction that* **MORA** *has frozen.* **NEEL, ELINORE,** *and* **ILLY** *are trying to get* **MORA**'s *attention to tell her she is frozen. Then the three of them try to run around the room seeing if they can get a better signal or*

call her on a different phone. Eventually they go off, looking to see if they can get a better signal elsewhere.)

But it feels, like it feels like maybe some of the pieces of my life are finally coming together and I just... I want to spend a little more time with her here. I'm getting to know the local communities here and there's this election coming up and I'm thinking about getting involved, which Srey is really supportive of...and I'm sorry, Illy, Neel, I know we said we'd do this together—but I have to do this on my own. And you'll each understand when you go through this too.

...

Fam? Are you still there? Man, I really do need to get a better pocket Wi-Fi.

ACT THREE: Dramatic Drama

Scene i

(In the darkness, there is loud, ferocious chirping that grows louder and louder. Lights up on **MANY BIRDS**, *who are completely at home.)*

*(***A BIRD*** *from before is* **BIRD 1**.*)*

BIRD 3. Attention, please.

(Spotlight on **BIRD 3**.*)*

Bird council meeting
Begin! Begin!

ALL BIRDS. Begin! Begin!

BIRD 5. Attention, please!

(Spotlight on **BIRD 5**.*)*

We die we die we die
Because because
Air air
Poof poof poof
Because because
Illy buy sky
Illy buy sky
So very birds

ALL BIRDS. Very birds!

BIRD 1. Attention, please.

(Spotlight on **BIRD 1**.*)*

BIRD 1. Illy suspect
　　Suspect Illy
　　So we kill kill kill
　　Kill Illy
　　Then Illy mate sad
　　Humans sad forever
　　Birds safe forever
　　So very birds

ALL BIRDS. Very birds!

BIRD 4. Attention, please!

(Spotlight on **BIRD 4**.*)*

　　No kill no kill
　　If birds kill Illy
　　Illy mate kill birds
　　Then birds kill Illy mate
　　Illy mate's mate kill birds
　　No end no end
　　Cycle cycle
　　So very birds

ALL BIRDS. Very birds!

BIRD 2. Attention, please.

(Spotlight on **BIRD 2**.*)*

　　But then how peace?
　　Peace peace peace?
　　So very birds.

ALL BIRDS. Very birds!

BIRD 4. Change.

　　　　*(***ALL BIRDS*** start cheeping "change? change?
　　　　change?" at their own tempos and rhythms.)*

Attention, please!

> (**REST OF BIRDS** *quiet.*)

Change Illy
Make Illy See
See see see

BIRD 6. Attention, please!

> (*Spotlight on* **BIRD 6**.)

So you're saying in order for us to stop Illy from buying the sky and causing the bird disease that has been killing us, we have to make Illy understand what we are going through and change her mind?

How do change?

> (**ALL BIRDS** *repeat "How how how?" in different rhythms and times.*)

BIRD 2. Attention, please!

> (**REST OF BIRDS** *quiet.*)

Change!
Change change change
Change Illy mate
Illy mate bird
Then
Illy Illy Illy
See See See

REST OF BIRDS. Ahhhhhhh!
Illy mate bird
Illy mate bird
Change change change
See See See!

BIRD 3. Now is time
Funeral time.

ALL BIRDS. Funeral time!
Funeral time!

BIRD 3. We honor our dead birds
Names of dead birds
Dead bird names
Are:

Bird

Bird

Bird

Bird

Bird

Bird

Bird

And Bird.

We honor dead
Dead dead dead
With karaoke

ALL BIRDS. Karaoke! Karaoke!

BIRD 3. Press play
Play play play

>*(One of the **BIRDS** hits a button on an old cassette tape player maybe?)*

>*(A karaoke track starts to play.)*

>*(Perhaps the lyrics, which are just the word CHEEP repeated over and over again, are projected a la karaoke?)*

>*(The music starts, and where the melody and lyrics should begin, the **BIRDS** do not sing the melody, they start madly chirping and*

*squawking like realistic birds. They do this
until the karaoke track ends.)*

*(As soon as the track ends and the birds quiet,
we hear:)*

SREY. Thank you all so much for coming today.

*(Lights on **SREY**.)*

(She holds a mic.)

*(She stands in front of a funeral altar, topped
with a photo of **MORA** in a frame of flowers.)*

*(Except, perhaps, instead of a photo, it is the
actor playing **MORA**, her face frozen in the
frame of flowers. Like a ghost.)*

I am so sorry to have to meet so many of you under
such unfortunate circumstances.

I knew I had to come to America to bring Mora's ashes
to her family, and the Whistlers have been so gracious
in letting me participate in her memorial today.

I really wish you all could have witnessed Mora thrive
in Cambodia.

It was extraordinary the way she embraced the culture
and the people.

She even entered politics to try to create a bright future
for the country.

I thought I could at least share with you some
photographs of our few months together.

*(**SREY** gestures to an unseen slideshow.)*

(Or perhaps she gestures to the couch.)

This is Mora having a belated celebration for her
thirtieth birthday with some of the people in our town,
a few weeks after she landed—

*(Lights on **ILLY** and **NEEL** on the couch.)*

ILLY. Assassinated? What do you mean assassinated?

NEEL. That's just what Mora's birth mother's email says.

ILLY. You have to be a politician to be assassinated. Or, like, an activist.

NEEL. Like me.

*(Lights on **SREY**.)*

SREY. This is Mora crocheting with our elders—she was very popular with the older adults, because of her caring nature, as you can imagine—

*(Lights on **ILLY** and **NEEL** on the couch.)*

NEEL. Thank you, Srey, for bringing her ashes to us. Mom, this is Mora's birth mother.

ILLY. This woman is not Mora's birth mother—

*(Lights on **SREY**.)*

SREY. This is Mora showing some elementary school children how to bake the traditional American chocolate chip muffin—

*(Lights on **ILLY** and **NEEL** on the couch.)*

NEEL. Like I said yesterday, Mom, this is Mora's birth mother.

ILLY. This woman is not Mora's birth mother—

*(Lights on **SREY**.)*

SREY. This is Mora speaking at a rally for LGBTQIA+ rights—

*(Lights on **ILLY** and **NEEL** on the couch.)*

ILLY.	NEEL.
For the last time, you are not an activist, you just have a weird new bird obsession—	None of the environmental activists will let me into their organizations because I'm dating you—

*(Lights on **SREY**.)*

SREY. This is Mora leading a women's support group—

*(Lights on **ILLY** and **NEEL** on the couch.)*

ILLY. No, Mom, this woman is not the cleaning lady, this is Mora's birth mother—I mean, she's not—

*(Lights on **SREY**.)*

SREY. This is Mora speaking at a fundraiser—

*(Lights on **ILLY** and **NEEL** on the couch.)*

*(**ILLY** and **NEEL** are kissing and then **NEEL** pulls away.)*

ILLY.	NEEL.
	You can't keep doing that every time we argue! It's really hard to be with you if we can't fundamentally agree on—Are you even listening to me?? Illy!
Yes I can, I can do whatever I want, because I am the person who has a job and the person who is taking care of Mom and the memorial and the house renovation—	ILLY. I am saying I don't know how to be with you anymore—

*(Lights on **SREY**.)*

SREY. This is Mora learning how to drape a sampot—

*(Lights on **ILLY** and **NEEL** on the couch.)*

(A small bird chirps from somewhere and only **NEEL** *hears it.)*

NEEL. Huh?

(Lights on **SREY.***)*

SREY. This is Mora singing—

(Lights on the portrait of **MORA,** *whose mouth opens and out pours the song Neel played for the start of his journey in Act One, Scene v.*)*

(Lights on **SREY.***)*

This is Mora—

(Lights on **ILLY** *and* **NEEL** *on the couch.)*

ILLY. Mora is the kind of person who calls us to come pick her up when she's drunk at a 7-Eleven at two a.m. like once a month because she got dumped or fired or both. This Cambodian Evita that Srey is describing is not Mora—Srey is probably not even Cambodian—she doesn't even look Cambodian—she looks—she looks— honestly she looks amazing, like, she's very beautiful— but she could be lying about everything—Mora might not even be dead!

NEEL. Illy... I know this is...hard but... I mean, you saw those photos—

(Lights on **SREY.***)*

SREY. And this is... yes. In the Cambodian Buddhist tradition, it is customary to have a funeral procession where the casket is brought from the home to the

---

* A license to produce *Regretfully, So the Birds Are* does not include a performance license for any third-party or copyrighted music. Licensees should create an original composition or use music in the public domain. For further information, please see the Music and Third-Party Materials Use Note on page iii.

temple. This transparent glass casket we picked for Mora is very trendy right now, especially for celebrities. She looks so peaceful here, doesn't she? I wanted to make sure she looked beautiful in her death since she was going to be seen by so many people, so when I was cleaning her body for the funeral, I was going to put make-up on her but... *(She gets overwhelmed.)* she was already...so beautiful...just the way she was...

(She composes herself.)

Next we will hear from Mora's other mother, the woman who raised her: Elinore Whistler.

*(**SREY** exits. A pause. Then **ILLY** runs to the altar.)*

ILLY. So sorry everyone, my mother just needs a moment.

*(**ILLY** runs back off.)*

*(**ELINORE** walks on slowly and stands elsewhere, as if at the altar.)*

(She holds the mic.)

(From offstage.) Mom?! MOM!

ELINORE. Thank you all so much for coming today.
This is me, Elinore, trying to give a speech at Mora's memorial.
But it's not going so well.
First I refuse to go on and then I run away and then I start sobbing and then I forget my speech—
It's a disaster, really.
And Illy is really trying to make everything seem okay—
But it's not okay.
I'm not okay.
Even before the dementia.

*(**ILLY** runs back to the altar.)*

ILLY. So sorry folks, she just needs a few more seconds—

(**ILLY** *runs back off.*)

ELINORE. I'm not saying this excuses anything
But if menstrual cycles were studied more thoroughly
They would have figured out my endometriosis much
earlier.
And I wouldn't have let the doctors close up my ovaries.
And I wouldn't have been put on Vicodin.
And I wouldn't have had to battle an opioid addiction
my entire life.
And I wouldn't get into a state
Of such intense paranoia during an opioid high,
That I hear Illy and Neel fooling around in the house
And mistake them for my husband's mistresses.
And all that rage I've had inside me against my husband
bubbles over.
And I run to his office and set fire to him.
But then I remember—oh right, his mistresses died
years ago.
In that dorm fire that tragically killed all those students.
Those deaths really changed him.
Made him a more dedicated father.
Which really made me resent him more.
Being a bad husband and a bad professor made him a
better parent?
How the hell is that fair?

(**ILLY** *runs back to the altar.*)

ILLY. Apologies, so sorry, not quite sure what's gotten into
her, she'll be right back—

(**ILLY** *runs back off.*)

ELINORE. And that's why when my children asked me why
I burned him,
I finally told them about their father's nasty past behavior.

But I embellished a little...
I said he's had dozens of affairs with his Asian students
And that they were still going on—
Even though it was only two affairs.
And they stopped a long time ago.

>	(**ILLY** *runs back to the altar.*)

ILLY. Thank you for your patience folks, just a few— *(Sees something offstage.)* No, Srey, don't touch her!

>	(**ILLY** *runs back off.*)

ELINORE. I wish I could tell Illy that it's okay.
It's okay that everything is not okay.
That's just how it is sometimes.
But.
It's so hard, you know?
When someone reminds you of everything you're not?
This isn't what my speech would have been at Mora's memorial, though.
(Chuckles.) That would be crazy.

>	(**ELINORE** *starts to exit but then:*)

Although, you know. Maybe it would have been.
I am a little crazy.

>	(**ELINORE** *exits.*)

>	(**ILLY** *to the altar with her viola.*)

ILLY. Apologies, everyone. We are actually going to skip ahead to...

>	(*We hear a bird cheeping somewhere.*)

Excuse me, I'm sorry, one moment, not sure why there's a bird in here...

>	(*She runs offstage trying to look for the bird.*)

NEEL. Thank you all so much for coming today.

> (**NEEL** *appears somewhere else, as if he's at the altar, with a mic.*)

This is me, Neel, trying to give a speech at Mora's memorial.
I'm trying to tell a story about how Mora took me to the zoo when we were younger.
And how we got kicked out of the zoo because Mora was being Mora.
And how she took me for ice cream after.
And how it was one of the most exciting days I'd ever had.
But Illy's not letting me tell this story.
She's trying to shoo me out of here,
Because she thinks I'm just a bird—
And.
I am.
Just a bird.
See, earlier I was trying to write my speech
When a flock of birds surround me and are like:

ALL BIRDS. Illy mate bird
Illy mate bird
Change change change
See see see

NEEL. And I tell them, "Yes I am Illy's mate but I'm not a bird," and they ask:

ALL BIRDS. Change change change?

NEEL. And I ask them to say that again—

ALL BIRDS. Change change change?

NEEL. And again—

> (*The **BIRDS** start cheeping "Change change change" in very differing rhythms and tones that sound very bird-ish.*)

And then something clicks, I realize, "Wait are you guys singing?"

ALL BIRDS. *(Very off-key.)* Sing sing sing
Bird speak is bird sing

NEEL. The birds are tone-deaf.
I am tone-deaf.

ALL BIRDS. Illy mate
Change change change!
Change to bird?
Change to bird?
Change to bird?
Yes?

NEEL. *(To* **BIRDS**.*)* Yes.
I will change into a bird.
(To audience.) Tone-deaf.
Regretfully, so the birds are.
Regretfully, so am I.
You know, to the non-tone-deaf, we sound like:

(**ALL BIRDS** *start chirping and squawking.*)

NEEL. But to our tone-deaf ears we sound like:

(The karaoke track from before plays.)

(**ALL BIRDS** *beautifully sing on-key the karaoke song from before.*)

ALL BIRDS. *(Sing.)*
CHEEP CHEEP CHEEP CHEEP CHEEP CHEEP CHEEP
CHEEP CHEEP CHEEP CHEEP CHEEP
CHEEP CHEEP CHEEP CHEEP
CHEEP CHEEP CHEEP CHEEP CHEEP CHEEP
CHEEP CHEEP CHEEP CHEEP CHEEP
CHEEP CHEEP CHEEP CHEEP CHEEP CHEEP CHEEP

*(And through the song, **NEEL**, who is also singing, becomes a **BIRD**, and is just one of many birds, indistinguishable from the rest.)*

*(**ILLY** re-enters with her viola and stands next to the funeral altar, out of breath.)*

ILLY. Hi everyone—
So, so, SO sorry about all of that—
Thank you all so much for coming today.
...Honestly I wasn't prepared for this many people to attend...
Although...now that I'm looking at you all I think most of you dated her at one point?
Anyway...
I have composed a viola piece for Mora.
And it will conclude our memorial today.
There will be a reception to follow—
Uh, except there will be no ice because the plumber was finally supposed to come this morning and didn't show.
So.
BYOI.

*(**ILLY** takes a position to play the viola.)*

(She plays a note or two but it's terrible.)

I'm so sorry, let me start again.

*(**ILLY** takes a deep breath.)*

*(**ILLY** tries to play again but it still fails.)*

So sorry, excuse me.
I promise, I've won awards for this for a reason.

(She weakly attempts to laugh.)

(She takes a position to play.)

(She is frozen for a moment.)

(It seems her hand starts shaking.)

CAM THE SNOWMAN(???). Are you all right?

> (**ILLY** *gasps and looks at* **CAM THE SNOWMAN(???)**, *who has always been here.*)

> (**CAM THE SNOWMAN(???)** *takes off his snowman head.*)

It's Illy, right? It's been a while—I'm the plumber, I'm... I'm here to fix the fridge's ice maker?

ILLY. Oh, sorry, um... you were supposed to come this morning.

THE PLUMBER. You said seven p.m.?

ILLY. What, no, I said seven... *(She scrolls through her texts to see.)* Oh shit. I wrote seven p.m... shit, wow, I'm sorry. And we kept delaying your appointment too...

THE PLUMBER. About half a year, yeah.

ILLY. OH MY GOD.

THE PLUMBER. You'd be surprised how often it happens. How's your dad doing?

ILLY. He died.

THE PLUMBER. Oh, I'm so sorry.

ILLY. Don't be. My mom set him on fire because it turned out he slept with his students and maybe also had an Asian fetish, so we don't even—well I don't like to talk about him. It would have been better if he just melted away like a [**THE PLUMBER.** Candle.] snowman—oh a candle, yeah, that works too. Anyway, um, to make up for the delay, maybe I could hire you to do the plumbing for my new home? It's in the sky, so obviously plumbing is a little more complicated—

THE PLUMBER. Oh... you... you're part of the human-to-sky migration?

ILLY. Yeah, my plot is not too far from here, you can kinda see it if you look—

THE PLUMBER. Sorry, I'm uh… I'm happy to fix the ice maker of your house here but uh… I sort of don't do sky homes? As in I, uh, I'm…ethically…against the human-to-sky migration thing? I mean… I'm sure you've heard the way it's really harming our environment…?

ILLY. …

I don't have anything.

Okay?

I don't have a dad, or a sister, and my partner who is also my brother has left me so I don't have either of those things, and I never had a mother who loved me, and now I have even less of one because of her stupid dementia, and my parents took away from me any sense of heritage or culture the moment I was born, so I really don't need a stranger to tell me how I can't have the sky because I deserve to have one thing that is mine and blank and untouched and something I can make something out of, okay? OKAY?

THE PLUMBER. …Wow… I'm so sorry… Jesus H. That's a lot of stuff to have happened to you… did you say, though… that your partner is…like, you were dating your brother? And everyone was like…okay…? With that?

ILLY. It's fine we're not blood-related—fuck.

THE PLUMBER. Oh, uh… but don't you two have the same…? I mean, I know your sister is adopted but aren't you and your brother…? You were the two babies that miraculously survived that dorm fire that tragically killed all those students, including both your biological mothers, who your dad had—Not to know your whole business, it was just really big news in the neighborhood at the time—

ILLY. Wait.

Sorry.

Stop.

Wait.

WAIT.

…

Wait we're…
You're telling me that we're…
You're telling me Neel and I are…
Neel and I are…
Neel and I are white?

THE PLUMBER. …Sorry I didn't mean to, uh… I just figured you had to have known? I mean you look…half…?

ILLY. …

…

…

…

…

I'm so sorry.
I have to, um.
Go?
Can you come back in…
Actually you don't have to come back.
I'll pay you for the—
I just really have to—
Oh no—
I think I have to go on a—

> (*The intro of the same song Neel played in Act One, Scene v starts to play.**)
>
> (**ILLY** *prepares to go on a journey.*)

---

* A license to produce *Regretfully, So the Birds Are* does not include a performance license for any third-party or copyrighted music. Licensees should create an original composition or use music in the public domain. For further information, please see the Music and Third-Party Materials Use Note on page iii.

(She grabs a neck pillow and a suitcase.)

(Is it Mora's neck pillow? Is it Neel's suitcase?)

ILLY. Attention, please.

*(A spotlight on **ILLY**.)*

I'm off to Guangzhou, China.
The U.S. Consulate in Guangzhou, China has processed
every intercountry adoption from China since 1992.
There have been over 83,000 immigrant visas issued
by the U.S. to Chinese adoptees since 1992.
I am going to find my sister's birth mother—oops,
I mean, first mother—
That's the preferred nomenclature—
I have this great plan to find Mora's first mother—
I'm gonna walk up to every person in China.
And I'm gonna say...
I mean.
I have this great plan to find Mora's first mother—
I'm gonna go to the U.S. Consulate in Guangzhou,
China and I'm gonna say,
"Hi. I'm sorry to interrupt your day.
But I was wond..."
...
I mean.
I have this great plan.
To find myse...
...
...
I mean I have this great plan to find mys-
I have this great plan to find mys-
I have this great plan to find mys-
I have this great...
I have...this...
I have...

(She looks at what she has.)

...

...

...

...

I have—

The End

(The curtain call must be a jig. And when I say jig, I don't mean a mid-sixteenth-century British folkdance. I mean a casually choreographed dance of jubilation set to pop music.)*

---

* A license to produce *Regretfully, So the Birds Are* does not include a performance license for any third-party or copyrighted music. Licensees should create an original composition or use music in the public domain. For further information, please see the Music and Third-Party Materials Use Note on page iii.

I Bought the Sky

from *Regretfully, So the Birds Are*

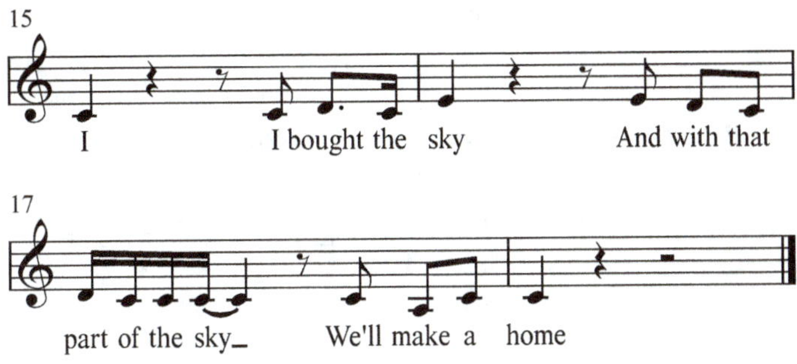

The Daisy Will Wilt

from *Regretfully, So the Birds Are*

Music & Lyrics by JULIA IZUMI
Transcribed by Grace Oberhofer

♩= 144

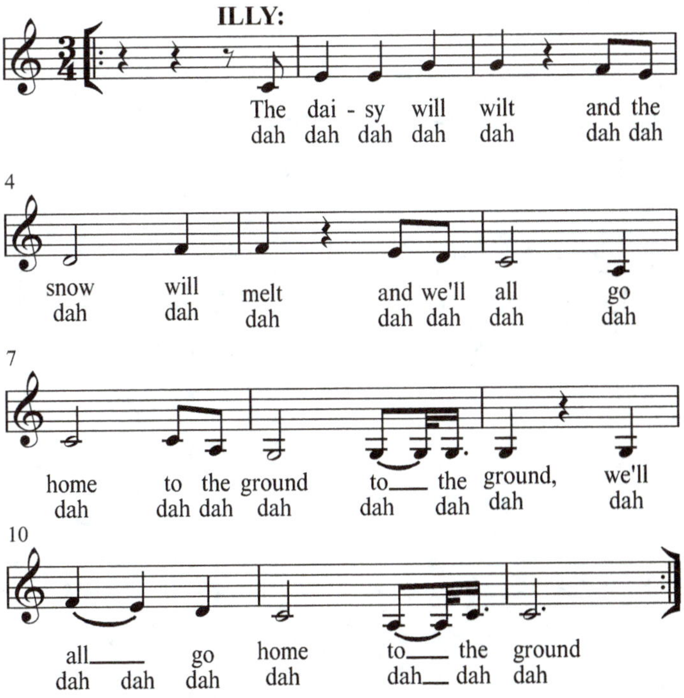

Bird Anthem

from *Regretfully, So the Birds Are*

Music & Lyrics by JULIA IZUMI
Transcribed by Grace Oberhofer

$\dotted{} = 75$

Bird Doo-Wop (can play with tempo)

www.ingramcontent.com/pod-product-compliance
Lightning Source LLC
Chambersburg PA
CBHW071929130726
47909CB00014B/2829